Albie
and the
Big Race

FOR ALBEMARLE
THE BEST LITTLE BOY IN THE WORLD

More wild stories by Andy Cutbill:
Albie
Albie and the Space Rocket

Andy Cutbill and Cosgrove Hall have created the television series, *Albie*, for CITV; winner of:

•

Best Children's Series, British Animation Awards
Canal Grande Prize for Best European Programme, Cartoons on the Bay Festival, Italy
B+ Prize for Best Young Writer, in association with BBC Resources
Best Animated Children's Series Episode, Chicago International Children's Film Festival
Best Children's Series, Bradford International Film Festival
Best TV Series, Annecy International Festival
Shortlisted for a BAFTA Award, 2003

•

First published in hardback in Great Britain by HarperCollins Children's Books in 2004
First published in paperback in 2004

1 3 5 7 9 10 8 6 4 2
ISBN-13: 978-0-00-780972-1 (PB)

HarperCollins Children's Books is a division of HarperCollins Publishers Ltd.

Text copyright © Andy Cutbill 2004
Illustrations copyright © Andy Cutbill/Ripping Gags and HarperCollins Publishers Ltd 2004

Based on the television series *Albie* © Cosgrove Hall Films Ltd

The author and illustrators assert the moral right to be identified
as the author and illustrators of the work.
A CIP catalogue record for this title is available from the British Library.

Visit our website at: www.harpercollinschildrensbooks.co.uk

Printed and bound in Malaysia

To find out more about Andy Cutbill's books,
visit his website: www.rippinggags.co.uk

Albie
and the
Big Race

by Andy Cutbill

ILLUSTRATIONS BY
Andy Cutbill and Mark Stacey

HarperCollins *Children's Books*

It was just another sunny afternoon.

Albie was returning home

from school when…

Beep! Beep!

Whooosh… A couple of camels in a shopping trolley knocked him clean off his feet.

"Excuse me!" said Albie angrily.

"Sorry," called one of the camels.

"Can't stop," shouted the other.

And they disappeared straight through the front door into Albie's house.

Albie climbed to his feet and stomped after them. As he entered the house he found…

…the hallway was bustling with activity. There were moose sipping tea, water buffalo eating sandwiches…

and elephants munching on the curtains.

"Excuse me, could you tell me what's

going on?" Albie asked.

"Don't you know?"
said a hippo, offering
him a pickled onion.

"Today is the Annual Smokin' Wheels Speed Convention," said a moose.

"Do you have a pair of smokin' wheels?" asked an elephant politely.

"No," said Albie.

"Well you'd better have these." And he handed Albie a pair of roller skates.

"B-b-b-but… these skates belong to my sister, Mary!" exclaimed Albie.

"Yup," said the hippo.

"But she'll do her nut when she finds out you've got them."

"We haven't got them," said the animals.

"*You* have!"

Suddenly a voice crackled over a loudspeaker.

"All drivers to the starting line!"

Albie was swept through the back door, only to find…

…the most **enormous** racetrack he'd ever seen.

It was made from doors, floorboards, beams and rafters.

"Where did you get all this wood from?" Albie asked an elephant.

"We *borrowed* it," said the elephant, winking.

Meanwhile, inside, Mary had just got home from school.

She was about to go upstairs to her room, when she noticed…the entire staircase was missing.

"ALLLBBBBiiiiiiiiiiiiiiieeeeeeeeeeeeeeee!" she screamed. "Where's the staircase?"

Behind the house, the race was starting.

"On your marks!"

yelled a rhinoceros.

There were penguins on a hostess trolley,
a moose on a television set and a herd
of zebras inside a grandfather clock!

Albie shuffled into line…

"Get set!"

shouted the rhino…

…and soared over terrific jumps.

But suddenly, Albie spotted a flash of red hair through the kitchen window. "Mary!" he gasped.

"ABANDON THE RACE!"

screamed the animals.

But Albie couldn't stop!

And just as Mary walked out into the garden...

Wallop!

...she promptly joined the race.

"What on earth are you doing with my roller skates?" Mary screamed angrily. Albie couldn't see where he was heading.

"An elephant gave them to me!" he shouted. "The same elephant that pinched all these floorboards I suppose?" yelled Mary.

"No," wailed Albie. "I think the pesky penguins took those."

And he crashed through the winner's tape.

Mary was catapulted

straight on to…

…a runaway grand piano!

"But Albieeee,"

Mary screamed…

…as the piano

hurtled towards

the back door.

"A house with no doors, beams

or floorboards is very likely to…"

WOOOSH

RUMBLE

"Fall down?" asked Albie.

"Oh flips," said Albie.